Rabbit and the Moon

by Douglas Wood   Illustrated by LESLIE BAKER

ALADDIN PAPERBACKS
New York London Toronto Sydney Singapore

AUTHOR'S NOTE

This retelling is based on a beautiful Cree legend I first discovered in a collection by Natalia M. Belting called *The Long-Tailed Bear* (Bobbs-Merrill Co., Indianapolis, 1961). The Cree are an Algonquian people of the northern plains and north woods of Saskatchewan and Manitoba.

Among native peoples of North America, Rabbit–sometimes known as Great Rabbit, the Great Hare, the Magic Hare, the trickster-hero–plays a vital role in traditional lore. The Micmac, Passamaquoddy, Lakota, Iroquois, Ojibwe, and many others tell of Rabbit. Traditional stories of the Creek and Cherokee are the origin of the beloved "Brer Rabbit" tales of the South. And many legends tell of a rabbit on the moon. There are also ancient rabbit-on-the-moon stories from India, Japan, and Central America.

The Whooping Crane depicted in this book is a spectacular, but now extremely rare, bird. As of this writing, only about 230 remain in the wild, and extensive efforts are underway to continue to increase their population and protect their habitat. To learn more about cranes, you can contact the International Crane Foundation, P.O. Box 447, Baraboo, Wisconsin 53913.

First Aladdin Paperbacks edition June 2001
Text copyright © 1998 by Douglas Wood
Illustrations © 1998 by Leslie Baker
ALADDIN PAPERBACKS
An imprint of Simon & Schuster
Children's Publishing Division
1230 Avenue of the Americas
New York, NY 10020
Also available in a Simon & Schuster Books for Young Readers hardcover edition.
Designed by Lucille Chomowicz.
The text for this book was set in Hiroshige.
The illustrations were rendered in pencil and transparent watercolor
on 90-pound Arches cold-press watercolor paper.
Printed in Hong Kong
10 9 8 7 6 5 4 3 2 1
The Library of Congress has cataloged the hardcover edition as follows:
Wood, Douglas, 1951 - Rabbit and the moon / story by Douglas Wood ; illustrations by Leslie Baker.
p.   cm.
Summary: Crane helps Rabbit fulfill his dream of riding across the sky to the moon.
ISBN: 0-689-80769-4 (hc.)   1. Cree Indians-Folklore.   2. Tales-Prairie Provinces.
[1. Rabbit (Legendary character)-Legends. 2. Cree Indians-Folklore. 3. Indians of North America-Canada-Folklore.
4. Folklore-Canada.] I. Baker, Leslie A., ill.
II. Title E99.C88W65 1988 398.2'089'973-dc20 [E] 96-31651
ISBN: 0-689-84304-6 (Aladdin pbk.)

To Eric, who reaches for his dreams.
—D. W.

To all those teachers who help make
children's dreams come true.
—L. B.

*O*nce, long ago—in the morning of the world—there was a rabbit. He was like most other rabbits, except for one thing. He had a dream. It was the sort of dream that will not go away, that is there when you are asleep *and* awake, and tugs at you even when you are trying to think of something else.

The dream that tugged at Rabbit—tugged so hard it made his ears wiggle and his nose twitch—was the dream of riding upon the moon at night, far above the Earth.

Rabbit had always known the Earth from very near. His nose knew the scents of leaves and mushrooms and fresh green grass. His ears knew the sounds of Brother Mouse rustling and Cricket singing. But Rabbit's eyes longed to see the Earth from high above—to see the darkness of the forests and the sparkling of the waters.

Rabbit had always known the moon from far away. It drew close only in the reflecting pool where he drank at night. He longed to see how bright it truly was, and how it slipped past the stars as it crossed the sky.

It would be the grandest thing he could imagine—to ride the shining moon among the stars and to see the beauty of the Earth below.

So Rabbit watched the moon. He watched it when it dangled like a bear's claw over the spruces; watched it when it shone with only half its light like a mushroom's cap; and watched it when it hung as round and full as Old Porcupine's belly. He watched it rise up in the evening, over the eastern edge of the world. He watched as the moon climbed above him and moved across the night sky. Rabbit watched the moon until the sun filled the sky with light, and he could see the moon no longer.

And Rabbit thought to himself, "If I go to the edge of the world, where the moon first comes up, I will be able to catch ahold of it as it rises."

So Rabbit went to the place where he had seen the moon come up, and when it began to rise, big and round and yellow, Rabbit reached out to catch it. He couldn't reach it. He jumped as high as he could jump. Still, he couldn't reach it.

But Rabbit did not give up.

"Tomorrow night I will climb to the top of the highest hill," said Rabbit. "Surely I'll be able to reach the moon from there."

The next evening Rabbit waited on top of the highest hill he could find, and as the moon began to rise he stretched out to touch it. It was too far away. He jumped and jumped. The moon rose higher still, and Rabbit could not reach it.

But Rabbit did not give up.

"The only way I am going to reach the moon," Rabbit said, "is to fly there."

Now in those long-ago times, rabbits were not very good fliers. So the next morning, Rabbit went to the biggest flying bird he could find and said, "Sister Eagle, I would like to ride on the moon, but I cannot reach it. Will you take me there?"

"No," said Eagle, "I cannot take you to the moon. It is too far, and I am too busy."

Rabbit found the Red-tailed Hawk. "Brother Hawk, can you carry me to the moon?" asked Rabbit.

"No," said Hawk. "I have more important things to do. I cannot take you."

Rabbit went to Owl and Snow Goose, to Heron and Osprey and
Pelican, but none of the great birds would carry him to the moon.
Still, Rabbit did not give up.

Instead, he went to the small birds—Chickadee and Nuthatch and Song Sparrow, Brown Creeper and Kinglet, and all the tiny birds of the forest. Perhaps together they could carry him to the moon. But the small birds only laughed. "We cannot take you to the moon," they said. "You are too big, and the moon is too far away."

Rabbit went away by himself and sat very still. His ears drooped. His nose barely twitched at all. As hard as he had tried, he could not find a way to reach the moon. For the first time, he was ready to give up.

Then Rabbit heard a voice behind him say, "I will carry you to the moon, Rabbit."

Rabbit jumped with surprise. He turned around and saw that there was one great flying bird he had forgotten to ask—Crane.

Crane had noticed how hard Rabbit had tried to reach his dream, how bravely he had struggled. Crane remembered his own dream of learning to fly, and how others had helped. He decided he would help Rabbit.

Crane said, "Meet me tomorrow on top of the high hill, Rabbit, and I will fly you to the moon."

The next day Rabbit was so excited that he was waiting on top of the hill by noontime. He waited and waited as the sun moved slowly across the sky. Finally, just as the sun slipped down in the west and the moon rose in the east, Crane swooped in on his great wings.

"Hold tight to my legs, Rabbit," said Crane, "and I will carry you to the moon."

Rabbit held on as tightly as he could, and Crane began to rise into the sky. Rabbit was heavy and it was hard for Crane to carry him. But he flapped his great wings and slowly they climbed higher and higher.

Once Rabbit looked down at the earth, now small and far away. He felt a lump in his throat. He closed his eyes and held on even tighter. Rabbit's paws hurt. It was hard to hold on. But Rabbit did not give up.

Finally Rabbit felt something under his hind feet. "It's all right, Rabbit," said Crane. "We are on the moon. You can . . . let . . . go . . . of my legs now."

Slowly Rabbit let go. His paws were stiff and sore and tinged red with blood. But as he opened his eyes wide and began to look around, he forgot how sore his paws were. For what Rabbit saw was even more grand than what he had dreamed!

The stars glowed like fireflies in a summer meadow, so
close he could almost touch them. And he could see all the Earth
below—green and blue and beautiful, with white clouds billowing in the
skies and great waters cradling the land.

Rabbit filled up his eyes with the beauty of the earth, and tried hard
to keep his ears from trembling.

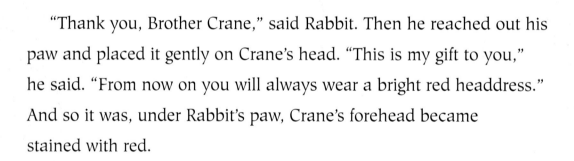

"Thank you, Brother Crane," said Rabbit. Then he reached out his
paw and placed it gently on Crane's head. "This is my gift to you,"
he said. "From now on you will always wear a bright red headdress."
And so it was, under Rabbit's paw, Crane's forehead became
stained with red.

Then Crane noticed that he felt a little . . . strange. His head did not hurt. His stomach felt good. His wings still worked. But his legs! Before his journey to the moon, Crane's legs were like those of the other birds—just the right size to carry him about. But now Crane's legs were long and thin, stretched out from carrying Rabbit to the moon.

And so it is today . . . Crane still walks on stretched-out legs, much longer than the legs of other birds. He is tall and proud, and he still wears a red headdress.

And Rabbit? Some night, when the moon is round and full like Old Porcupine's belly, look very closely. For you can still see Rabbit there, riding across the night sky.